Garlic...the Root of it All

Judy Meghnagi

iUniverse, Inc.
New York   Bloomington

iUniverse books may be ordered through booksellers or by contacting:

iUniverse
1663 Liberty Drive
Bloomington, IN 47403
www.iuniverse.com
1-800-Authors (1-800-288-4677)

Because of the dynamic nature of the Internet, any Web addresses or links contained in this book may have changed since publication and may no longer be valid. The views expressed in this work are solely those of the author and do not necessarily reflect the views of the publisher, and the publisher hereby disclaims any responsibility for them.

ISBN: 978-1-4401-2315-3(sc)
ISBN: 978-1-4401-2316-0(ebook)

Printed in the United States of America

iUniverse rev. date: 07/07/2009

Crushed garlic may be used in place of whole garlic in any recipe, just use half of the amount listed.

Ground turkey may be used in place of ground beef in meat recipes.

For all recipes t=teaspoon

T=tablespoon

Sauces

Basic Tomato Sauce

1 large chopped onion

2 medium diced tomatoes

10 garlic cloves-chopped

olive oil

1T fresh or dried rosemary

1 T fresh cilantro (optional)

1 t basil

1 t oregano leaves

1 t parsley leaves

1 can-28 oz crushed tomatoes

1 T balsamic vinegar

salt and pepper

1. Use a large frying pan-heat on low/medium

2. Saute onion, garlic and tomato in olive oil to cover pan

3. Cook until vegetables are soft

4. Add seasonings and crushed tomatoes with vinegar

5. Next add salt and pepper to taste and simmer on low for two hours or longer

6. Serve over your favorite pasta

Bean and Vegetable Pasta

olive oil

6 garlic cloves-chopped

1 small bunch of arugula

14 ½ oz. can diced tomatoes

1-16 oz can white beans-drained and rinsed

1/3 cup white wine

10 basil leaves

salt and pepper

1. Heat olive oil in large frying pan-cover bottom of pan

2. Saute garlic on low until softened

3. Add arugula-cook until wilted

4. Next add tomatoes, beans, wine and basil leaves

5. Cook on low/simmer for 1 hour and toss with cooked spaghetti

6. Add salt and pepper to taste

Broccoli and Garlic Pasta

1 pound of cooked pasta

olive oil

4 large bunches of fresh broccoli

10 chopped garlic cloves

salt and pepper

1 t vegetable broth-powder

crushed red pepper

paprika

1. Use a medium size frying pan and cover bottom with olive oil

2. Chop up tops of broccoli and discard bottoms

3. Saute broccoli with garlic until softened

4. Add salt and pepper to cover and mix it up

5. Next add vegetable powder, sprinkle red pepper and paprika and stir together

6. Add to pasta in large bowl and blend all ingredients

Fresh Homemade Tomato Sauce

16 whole cloves of garlic

21 plum tomatoes-chopped in quarters

2 onions-chopped

2 whole long hot peppers-remove stems

1 t each of cumin, salt and pepper

olive oil

1. Use a large pot with a cover
2. Cover bottom with oil
3. Add garlic, tomatoes, onions, peppers and seasonings
4. Cook on low/medium with no cover for 4 hours
5. Stir as needed and sauce will cook down low
6. Serve over cooked pasta or spread on fresh Italian bread
7. Sprinkle with fresh parmesan cheese if desired

Fresh Pesto Sauce

1 ½ cups fresh basil leaves (1 bunch)
4 garlic cloves
½ cup pine nuts, walnuts or cashews
½ cup olive oil
salt and pepper

1. Put all ingredients in a food processor and blend
2. Serve in bowls over cooked pasta
3. Stir in desired amount of pesto into each bowl
4. Cover and refrigerate leftover pesto

Pesto Tomato Sauce

olive oil

1 chopped onion

7 chopped garlic cloves

2 long hot peppers-remove seeds and chop

1 large carrot-peeled and chopped

1 T oregano

1 T Italian seasoning

½ cup white wine

2 large chopped tomatoes

1 T chicken or vegetable broth powder

1 T balsamic vinegar

1 T tomato paste

salt and pepper

2 T pesto sauce

1. Use a large frying pan and cover bottom with olive oil
2. Saute all vegetables until soft
3. Add seasonings, wine, tomatoes, broth powder, vinegar, tomato paste, plus salt and pepper to taste
4. Simmer for 1 hour
5. Cook 1 pound of pasta
6. Add 2 T fresh or store bought pesto to sauce and heat through
7. Put cooked pasta in large bowl
8. Add sauce and mix together

9. Serve warm and add a little more black pepper if desired

Sauce and Meatballs

Sauce

1 large chopped onion

6 garlic cloves-chopped

10 fresh basil leaves-cut up

4-8 oz cans of tomato sauce

¾ t salt

2 t black pepper

1 T oregano leaves

1 T thyme leaves

1. Use a large frying pan, cover bottom with olive oil and sauté onion, garlic and basil until soft

2. Add cans of sauce and all seasonings

3. Cook on low/simmer for one hour or longer

Meatballs

1 large chopped onion

4 chopped garlic cloves

1 ½ pounds ground beef

2 eggs

½ cup ketchup

1 cup seasoned bread crumbs

2 T soy sauce

1 t black pepper

1. Mix all ingredients and form small balls
2. Drop into sauce and simmer for 2-3 more hours
3. Serve over cooked spaghetti or make sandwiches with Italian bread or rolls

Sesame Pasta

1 pound of pasta-cooked and drained
1 bunch of scallions-chopped small
¼ cup light soy sauce
¼ cup seasoned rice vinegar
¼ cup sesame oil
3 cloves of garlic-crushed
black pepper
paprika

1. Mix soy sauce, rice vinegar, sesame oil and garlic
2. Add to cooked pasta in a large bowl
3. Mix up pasta with sauce
4. Add scallions, pepper and paprika to taste
5. Tastes great chilled or at room temperature

Soba Noodles

¼ cup creamy peanut butter

¼ cup light soy sauce

¼ cup fresh chopped cilantro

¼ cup seasoned vinegar

2 t fresh grated or powdered ginger

1/8 cup teriyaki sauce

½ t black pepper

2 crushed garlic cloves

10 oz package of soba noodles

1. Cook noodles as directed on package
2. Drain and reserve ¼ cup cooking water
3. Blend rest of ingredients in a large bowl
4. Add reserved water to mixture
5. Next add cooked noodles
6. Mix up and serve warm or cold with cilantro on top

Sun Dried Tomato Pasta

1 ½ cups sun dried tomatoes-chopped

olive oil

5 cloves of garlic-crushed

¼ - ½ t red pepper flakes

¼ cup fresh parsley-chopped

salt and pepper

1. Soak tomatoes in a bowl of hot water until soft-about 15 minutes
2. Use a medium size frying pan and put in olive oil to cover bottom
3. Saute garlic until soft and add drained tomatoes
4. Add red pepper flakes, salt and pepper to taste and cook on low-medium heat for about 15 minutes
5. Serve over cooked pasta and add parsley over the top

Tomato Pasta

olive oil

2 medium onions-chopped

6 garlic cloves-chopped

2-28 oz cans of whole peeled tomatoes

(drained and chopped)

¼ cup balsamic vinegar

10 fresh basil leaves

1 small bunch fresh parsley-chopped

salt and pepper

1. Cover bottom of large frying pan with olive oil
2. Saute onion and garlic until softened
3. Add tomatoes, vinegar, basil and parsley
4. Cook on low/simmer for 2 hours or longer
5. Sprinkle with salt and pepper to taste
6. Serve over cooked linguine or spaghetti

Vegetables

Butternut Squash and Spinach Saute

1 large butternut squash-peeled and chopped

1 large red onion-chopped

4 cloves of chopped garlic

olive oil

salt and pepper

1-6 oz package of fresh spinach

1 cup of fresh or dried cranberries

1. Use a large frying pan and cover bottom with oil
2. Saute squash, onion and garlic until soft
3. Season to taste with salt and pepper
4. Add spinach and cook until wilted
5. Add cranberries and cook a few minutes or mix up if dried

Cooked Cabbage

2 large onions

1 head of cabbage

1 cup fresh cranberries

4 garlic cloves

paprika

salt and pepper

olive oil

1 lemon

1. Use large fry pan and put oil to cover bottom
2. Cut up onions and garlic
3. Cook in oil until soft
4. Chop up cabbage and add to pan with cranberries and sauted onion and garlic
5. Season with salt, pepper and 2 T of paprika
6. Add juice of lemon, mix up and cook until all vegetables are soft

Garlic Mashed Potatoes

12 white baking potatoes

6 whole cloves of garlic

olive oil

salt and pepper

paprika

parsley, oregano or basil

1. Wash potatoes and cut in half
2. Put in a large pot of water covering the potatoes
3. Add garlic cloves and heat to boiling
4. Next simmer on low/medium with cover on halfway for about 30 minutes or until soft
5. Drain potatoes and garlic, then put in a large bowl
6. Use a potato masher or large spoon, add a drizzle of oil and mash
7. Add salt, pepper and paprika to cover top and mix up
8. Also add any green seasonings for flavor to cover top and blend

Greenbean Dish

2 T soy sauce

2 T water

1 t cornstarch

1 t brown sugar

1 t sesame oil

¼ t crushed red pepper flakes

fresh greenbeans

1. Blean ingredients above in a small bowl and set aside

olive oil

2 cloves of crushed garlic

1 t ginger

sesame seeds

2. Use medium size frying pan-saute desired amount of greenbeans in olive oil for 10 minutes on low-medium heat
3. Add garlic, ginger and soy sauce mixture
4. Saute for 10 more minutes
5. Stir up, sprinkle with sesame seeds and serve warm

Roasted Eggplant and Pepper Salad

1 large eggplant

3 large green peppers

2 garlic cloves-crushed

1 T lemon juice

1 T olive oil

salt and pepper

cayenne pepper

1. Preheat oven to 400 degrees
2. Pierce eggplant several times with a fork and bake whole on a foil lined tray for about 1 hour and let cool
3. Next broil peppers on same tray on high, turning often until skins are black on each side, about 20 minutes total
4. Put peppers in a bowl and let cool
5. Peel off the skins and remove the core and seeds
6. Dice the peppers and halve the eggplant
7. Remove the inside of the eggplant and mix with the peppers
8. Cut up into small pieces and add garlic, lemon juice, olive oil, salt, pepper and cayenne to taste
9. Taste and adjust seasonings if necessary
10. Serve cold or at room temperature with pitas, Italian bread or bagels

Roasted Garlic Heads

4 whole garlic heads
olive oil spray
olive oil
dried thyme
salt and pepper

1. Leave peel on garlic, chop a little bit off the tips of each head with a knife
2. Place tips up in a small pan sprayed with olive oil
3. Drizzle olive oil over heads and add thyme, salt and pepper to cover garlic
4. Cover heads with foil and seal shut
5. Roast in oven at 375 degrees for 45 minutes
6. Let cool and squeeze each head out on fresh Italian bread or bagels-spread and enjoy (great for curing a cold too)

Roasted Potatoes

1 large onion-chopped

10 cloves of garlic-cut in half

4 large sweet potatoes

4 large white potatoes

olive oil spray

olive oil

¼ cup fresh rosemary

salt and pepper

paprika

oregano

thyme

1. Spray a large baking pan with olive oil
2. Chop potatoes in quarters, leave peel on and put in pan
3. Add onion and garlic around potatoes
4. Drizzle olive oil over all vegetables
5. Add herbs and seasonings to cover (sprinkle all around)
6. Cover with foil and seal shut
7. Cook at 375 degrees for 1 hour

Vegetable Stew

2 chopped onions

4 chopped garlic cloves

2 sweet potatoes-chopped with peel on

1 can crushed tomatoes (28oz)

salt and pepper

½ cup raisins

1 15oz can chick peas (drained and rinsed)

1 green pepper-chopped

2 zucchini-cut in chunks (leave peel on)

¼ cup chopped fresh cilantro

olive oil

1. Use large frying pan and cover bottom with olive oil
2. Add onions, garlic, and sweet potatoes
3. Cook between low and medium heat until soft
4. Keep pan covered and add tomatoes
5. Season with salt and pepper
6. Next simmer on low for 15 minutes
7. Add raisins and chick peas and cook for 15 more minutes
8. Put in green pepper, ½ cup water, zucchini and cilantro
9. Simmer for 30 minutes and enjoy as a side dish or serve with rice

Veggie Couscous

olive oil

1 yellow squash

1 green zucchini

1 red onion

4 cloves of garlic

1 can chickpeas(drained)

1 t ground cumin

½ t coriander

¼ t ground red pepper

salt and pepper

2 cups cooked couscous

¼ cup chopped fresh parsley

1. Cover bottom of large frying pan with oil, sauté squash, zucchini, red onion and garlic until soft
2. Next stir in chick peas and spices until blended
3. Then stir in the couscous and cook until warm (about 10 min)
4. Add parsley on top and blend in some
5. This dish is great warm or may be served at room temperature

Chicken

Apricot Chicken

apricot preserves (16 oz)

1/3 cup gran marnier liquor

vegetable oil

1 onion-chopped

4 garlic cloves-chopped

1-8oz package mushrooms-chopped

4 white potatoes-chopped

salt and pepper

1 chicken cut up (3-4 lbs)

1. Use large pan, put oil to cover bottom and sauté all vegetables until softened (low/med heat)
2. Add preserves and gran marnier
3. Cook on low until preserves melt and mix in (about 30 min)
4. Use large baking pan and put chicken pieces in and pour sauce mixture over top
5. Sprinkle salt and pepper over chicken mixture
6. Bake at 350 degrees for 1 hour
7. Enjoy over wild rice if desired or any other type or rice

Chicken and Rice

1 onion chopped

6 cloves of garlic-chopped

1 – 3 lb chicken cut up

vegetable oil

4 red or green peppers-chopped

1 tomato-cut up

3 cups of brown rice

1 T vegetable or chicken boullion

1 T paprika

1 10oz box frozen lima beans

1 8oz package fresh mushrooms (optional)

salt and pepper

1. Sprinkle chicken with salt and pepper on both sides
2. Use large frying pan and add oil to cover bottom
3. Cook chicken until browned and put on a plate
4. Saute onion, garlic, peppers and tomato until soft
5. Add boullion, paprika, beans and mushrooms
6. Simmer for 10 minutes
7. Make rice in a different pot and mix into vegetables when done
8. Put rice mixture in large rectangle baking pan and lay chicken pieces over rice pushing them slightly into mixture
9. Sprinkle top with pepper and paprika and bake at 350 degrees for 30 minutes or until chicken is done

Company Chicken

2-8 piece cut up chickens

10 chopped garlic cloves

¼ cup dried oregano

salt and pepper to taste

½ cup red wine vinegar

½ cup olive oil

1 cup pitted prunes

½ cup green olives with pimento

½ cup capers-drained

6 bay leaves

1 cup brown sugar

1 cup white wine

¼ cup fresh parsley or cilantro-chopped

1. Use a large mixing bowl
2. Add first set of ingredients with chicken and mix together
3. Cover and marinate in refrigerator overnight
4. Put oven on 350 degrees
5. Place chicken in two rectangular baking pans and spoon marinade over top of chicken
6. Sprinkle chickens with sugar and pour wine around chicken pieces
7. Bake for one hour or until cooked through

8. Add parsley or cilantro (or both) to top of chicken
9. Serve warm or at room temperature

Garlic Chicken

3 heads of garlic

salt and pepper

thyme

olive oil

1 chicken cut up (8 pieces)

flavored bread crumbs

olive oil spray

paprika

rosemary (fresh or dried)

1. Heat oven to 450 degrees
2. Cut off top part of garlic bulbs (tips)
3. Put garlic on foil, drizzle with oil, salt, pepper and thyme
4. Wrap in foil and bake for 50 minutes
5. Let garlic heads cool and squeeze out garlic into a small bowl-remove all peel
6. Mash with 1 T fresh rosemary, salt, pepper and 1 t olive oil
7. Spray baking pan with olive oil and spread mixture across top of chicken pieces
8. Sprinkle paprika, pepper and bread crumbs across top of chicken and garlic spread
9. Cover evenly with olive oil spray and bake for 1 hour or until done

Indian Style Chicken

1 chicken-cut up (8 pieces)

1/3 cup cider vinegar

2 T molasses

2 sweet peppers (chopped-remove seeds)

2 T curry powder

3 crushed garlic cloves

8 red skin potatoes-cut in half

vegetable oil

1 chopped onion

½ t crushed red pepper flakes

2 chopped tomatoes

1-10oz box of frozen peas

salt and pepper

1. Use large bowl and mix first set of ingredients with chicken
2. Cover and marinate overnight in the refrigerator
3. Put vegetable oil in large frying pan
4. Saute onion and tomatoes with red pepper flakes
5. Add potatoes and cook until soft
6. Season with salt and pepper
7. Next add chicken and marinade
8. Cook at medium/low until chicken is cooked through
9. Simmer for 1 hour, add peas and cook for 1 more hour

Moroccan Style Chicken

olive oil

boneless or boned chicken (about 3 lbs total)

1 chopped onion

4 cloves of garlic-chopped

1 can (14 ½ oz) stewed tomatoes

salt and pepper

1 t dried oregano

½ t cumin

½ t cinnamon

1 zucchini-chopped with skin on

1 can (151/2 oz) chick peas-drained

½ cup raisins

1. Heat oil covering large frying pan
2. Saute onion, garlic and zucchini until soft
3. Add tomatoes and 5 seasonings listed
4. Put in chicken and brown on both sides
5. Simmer for 1 ½ hours
6. Add chick peas and raisins-simmer for 30 minutes
7. Enjoy with rice or couscous

Our Favorite Chicken Stew

olive oil

1 chopped onion

6 cloves of garlic-chopped

½ t turmeric

¾ t cinnamon

½ t ground cloves

2 bay leaves

2 cups vegetable broth

4 chicken legs & thighs (about 3 lbs total)

1 (14 ½ oz) can stewed tomatoes

1 can of green beans (15 ½ oz)-drained

1 can of butter beans(15 ½ oz)-drained

½ t salt

black pepper

1. Use a large frying pan, cover bottom with olive oil and sauté onion and garlic until soft
2. Add next 4 ingredients (seasonings)
3. Stir in broth, add chicken, tomatoes and bring to a boil
4. Mix in 2 beans, salt and pepper
5. Simmer for 2 hours
6. Serve in bowls over rice or couscous
7. This recipe can also be made using a crock pot

Soft Chicken Tacos

2-lbs boneless chicken

3 chopped garlic cloves

½ t ground red pepper

1 t shawarma seasoning (optional-middle eastern or Israeli grocery)

salt and pepper to taste

olive oil

1 chopped onion

1 can (15oz) red kidney beans

1 can (14 ½ oz) diced tomatoes

10 tortillas

1 avocado chopped

1 cup salsa

1. Use large frying pan, fill bottom with oil, cut chicken into chunks and sauté with seasonings listed
2. Add onion and garlic and cook until soft and chicken is done
3. Pour in drained beans and tomatoes with liquid
4. Stir together and simmer for two hours
5. Serve in warmed tortillas with salsa and avocado if desired (can also substitute steak pieces for chicken)

Sweet and Sour Chicken

1 ½ lbs boneless cubed chicken

vegetable oil

1 chopped green pepper

1 chopped red pepper

1 T cornstarch

¼ cup soy sauce

8 oz can pineapple chunks

3 T white vinegar

3 T brown sugar

½ t fresh or ground ginger

3 crushed garlic cloves

brown or white rice

1. Cook chicken pieces in large pan with oil, salt and pepper until browned
2. Add peppers, garlic and cook until softened
3. Mix cornstarch and soy sauce in pan with pineapple and juice
4. Next add vinegar, sugar and ginger-bring to a boil
5. Simmer for 30 minutes
6. Serve over rice

Meat

Bourekas

1 lb ground beef

vegetable oil

1 chopped onion

4 chopped garlic cloves

salt and pepper

1 t cinnamon

¼ cup water

3 T parsley

1 egg

1 package egg roll wrappers

1. Brown beef in 3 T vegetable oil
2. Add onion, garlic, salt and pepper, cinnamon, water and simmer for 45 minutes
3. Next add parsley, egg and mix well
4. Use wrappers, fold into triangles with mixture in each wrap and seal shut
5. Fill pan with oil and brown evenly on each side
6. Cook a few at a time and drain in colander using paper towels on a plate
7. Cool and enjoy warm or at room temperature

Chili Pasta

1 -16 oz box wagon wheel pasta or any type pasta
olive oil
1 chopped onion
5 chopped garlic cloves
1 chopped red pepper
1 ½ lbs ground beef
2 T chili powder
2 t cumin
½ t cinnamon
½ t salt
1 can stewed tomatoes (14 ½ oz)
1 can black beans (15 oz)

1. Use large frying pan and cover bottom with oil
2. Saute onion, garlic and pepper until soft
3. Add beef and cook until browned
4. Cover pan and drain grease by tilting into sink carefully or scoop with a ladle until most is removed
5. Add chili powder, cumin, cinnamon and salt
6. Next add stewed tomatoes and drained beans
7. Simmer for 30 minutes
8. Then add cooked pasta-use a large bowl and mix it up
9. Serve warm with salt and pepper if desired

Meat Stuffed Potatoes

6 white baking potatoes

½ lb ground beef

1 can corn or 1 frozen box (10 oz)

4 crushed garlic cloves

1 small chopped onion

1/8 cup olive oil

1 can stewed tomatoes (14 ½ oz)

1 small chopped green pepper

1 T chili powder

salt and pepper

1. Pierce potatoes with fork and microwave on high 16 minutes or until soft (rotate after 8 minutes) or bake at 350 degrees for 1 hour
2. Next use large frying pan and brown beef
3. Drain beef and add corn, garlic, onion, oil, tomatoes, pepper, chili powder, salt and pepper
4. Cook on low/medium until vegetables are soft, about 30 minutes with cover
5. Slit potatoes and spoon mixture over each one

Moroccan Meatballs in Tomato Sauce

Sauce:

olive oil

1 chopped onion

7 chopped garlic cloves

1 T tomato paste

2-28 oz cans crushed tomatoes

1 t cumin

1 T oregano

salt and pepper

1. Use oil to cover bottom of large pot
2. Add onion and garlic-saute until soft
3. Next add tomato paste and cook a little
4. Add crushed tomatoes and seasonings
5. Cook on low/simmer for 30 minutes

Meatballs:

1 ½ lbs ground beef

3 T seasoned bread crumbs

2 crushed garlic cloves

2 T fresh or dried parsley

1 t cumin

½ t allspice

¼ t cinnamon

salt and pepper

1. Put all ingredients in large bowl
2. Mix well and make into balls
3. Put meatballs in sauce and cook on low heat for 2 hours
4. Enjoy over pasta

Our Favorite Meatloaf

1 ½ lbs ground beef

½ cup ketchup

½ cup oatmeal

1 chopped onion

4 chopped garlic cloves

2 T fresh cilantro

2 T fresh or dried parsley

1 t ground cumin

1 T brown sugar

¼ t salt

¼ t pepper

2 eggs

1. Use a large bowl and add all ingredients (1/4 cup ketchup)
2. Mix well until blended
3. Use an 8x4 or 9x5 glass or metal pan
4. Spray with olive oil
5. Put mixture in pan and brush ¼ cup ketchup over top of loaf
6. Bake at 350 degrees for 1 hour
7. Slice and serve (great with mashed potatoes)

Pepper Steak Stir Fry

1 ½ lbs steak strips

1/3 cup worcestershire sauce

2 T brown sugar

1 T dijon mustard

4 crushed garlic cloves

1 chopped green or red pepper

1 small chopped onion

olive oil

salt and pepper

1. Marinate steak strips for 1 hour or longer with worcestershire sauce, brown sugar, mustard and 2 cloves of crushed garlic
2. Next use oil to cover large pan or wok
3. Saute pepper, onion, 2 more garlic cloves crushed, salt and pepper
4. Add steak with marinade and cook until done
5. Serve over rice

Sloppy Joes

3 lbs ground beef

2 chopped onions

10 chopped garlic cloves

1 chopped green pepper

salt and pepper

¾ cup ketchup

1 cup barbeque sauce

1 T seasoned rice vinegar

1 T spicy or regular mustard

1. Use large pan and brown beef until pink color disappears
2. Drain all liquid and use crock pot or large pan
3. Add onions, garlic, green pepper, salt and pepper to taste
4. In a separate bowl, mix ketchup, bbq sauce, worcestershire sauce, rice vinegar, mustard and add to crock pot or pan
5. Cook covered on low for 6 hours
6. Stir gently when done and throughout if desired
7. Serve on rolls or in bowls

Stuffed Flank Steak

1-2 lb flank steak

olive oil

1 chopped onion

4 chopped garlic cloves

4 oz cornbread stuffing

4 oz can green chilies

2 t chili powder

1 t cumin

¼ cup hot water

salt and pepper

kitchen twine

1 can Italian style stewed tomatoes (14 ½ oz)

1. Lay steak between 2 pieces of wax paper and pound with mallet to flatten
2. Use a large frying pan, cover bottom with oil, add onion and garlic-saute until soft
3. Put together stuffing, ½ can chilies, chili powder, cumin and hot water-mix well
4. Season steak with ¼ t salt and pepper
5. Set stuffing on top of steak and roll up the long sides and tie securely with twine
6. Use olive oil in same pan to coat lightly and add the steak roll

7. Brown on all sides and add stewed tomatoes, rest of chilies and bring to a boil, then simmer for 1 hour or until tender

8. Cut into slices, discard twine and add sauce from pan over slices

Stuffed Meatloaf

Stuffing:

1-10 oz frozen mixed vegetables

1 egg

2 T seasoned bread crumbs

1. Cook vegetables in microwave according to package directions
2. Let cool and mix with egg and crumbs

Meat mixture:

2 lbs ground beef

1 chopped onion

3 chopped garlic cloves

¼ cup ketchup

¼ cup oatmeal

¼ cup seasoned bread crumbs

1 egg

1 T worcestershire sauce

1 t black pepper

½ t salt

½ t garlic powder

olive oil spray

1. Combine meat mixture in large bowl and mix well
2. Use loaf pan and put olive oil spray in bottom
3. Put half meat mixture in pan, next add stuffing on top and then put in other half of meat mixture
4. Bake at 350 degrees for 1 hour
5. Serve with ketchup and mashed potatoes if desired

Fish

Almond Bread Crumb Fish

1 ½ lbs cod or tilapia

3 slices of bread (any type)

1/3 cup slivered almonds

3 garlic cloves

1/3 cup flavored bread crumbs

olive oil

1 lemon

1 t lemon zest (use peel)

olive oil spray

paprika

salt and pepper

1. Use a food processor-put bread, almonds, garlic and crumbs in and blend to puree
2. Drizzle ½ cup oil, juice of lemon and zest to processor and mix
3. Put fish in a large rectangle pan-sprayed with oil first
4. Cover with crumb mixture
5. Sprinkle with salt, pepper and paprika
6. Spray over whole fish with oil
7. Bake at 375 degrees for 45 minutes

Crispy Salmon

2 medium size wild salmon filets

non-dairy butter spray

2 crushed garlic cloves

¼ cup seasoned bread crumbs

¼ t salt

¼ t pepper

½ t onion powder

½ t oregano

½ t paprika

sesame oil

1. Use medium size oven ready frying pan-spray bottom with butter and drizzle sesame oil over top of spray
2. Crush garlic into pan and cook on low for 1-2 minutes
3. Mix up all seasonings on a plate
4. Dip and roll salmon pieces in mixture until covered
5. Cook on stove on med-high heat for 2 minutes or until browned on first side down
6. Next flip filets over and put same pan in oven at 400 degrees for six minutes or until cooked through
7. Fish should flake easily when done

Fish Pizzaiole

1 ½ lbs tilapia or cod

1 cup seasoned bread crumbs

1 T dried parsley

1 T dried oregano

1 can stewed tomatoes (14 ½ oz)

¼ cup olive oil

salt and pepper

1 chopped onion

4 chopped garlic cloves

olive oil spray

1. Mix crumbs and seasonings
2. Coat fish in mixture
3. Spray oil in large rectangle pan and lay fish on top
4. Spread onion, garlic and tomatoes over fish
5. Pour olive oil over fish and season with salt and pepper
6. Bake uncovered at 375 degrees for 45 minutes

Fresh Tomato Herb Fish

1 ½ lbs tilapia or cod

4 chopped plum tomatoes

¼ cup fresh basil

2 T marjoram leaves

1 chopped onion

2 T balsamic vinegar

olive oil

4 chopped garlic cloves

salt and pepper

1. Use large frying pan and cover bottom with oil
2. Saute tomatoes, onion and garlic until soft
3. Add basil, marjoram, vinegar, salt and pepper to taste
4. Cook covered on simmer for 30 minutes
5. Put fish on top of tomato herb mixture and cook on low/medium for 15 minutes or until done (you can cook the fish in cut up serving pieces)
6. Season with salt and pepper
7. Serve with rice or pasta

Garlic Tuna Teriyaki

tuna steaks (6-8)-average size

1 crushed garlic clove for each steak

¼ cup teriyaki sauce

black pepper

sesame oil

1. Rinse steaks in water and pat dry with paper towels
2. Lay steaks on large plate, crush garlic on top, pour teriyaki sauce over top and sprinkle with black pepper
3. Use a large frying pan-pour oil to cover bottom
4. Cook 1-2 minutes on each side or longer if desired (I like mine rare)

Horseradish Dill Salmon

2 lbs wild salmon-sliced thin

2 T light mayonnaise

4 T white horseradish

¼ cup fresh or dried dill

sea salt

black pepper

juice of 1 lemon

olive oil spray

1. Mix all ingredients
2. Spread on both sides of fish
3. Let sit for 20-30 minutes
4. Spray large pan with oil and sear 2-3 minutes each side or longer if necessary
5. Serve as an appetizer with crackers or as a main dish over rice

Lemon Fish

1 ½ lbs tilapia

olive oil

1 small chopped onion

4 chopped garlic cloves

2 diced medium tomatoes

3 oz chopped black olives

¼ cup dried or fresh parsley

¼ cup white wine

2 T capers

1 lemon

6 fresh basil leaves

salt and pepper

1. Use large frying pan with a cover
2. Cover bottom with oil
3. Saute onion and garlic until soft
4. Add tomatoes and olives and cook for 5 minutes or until tomatoes soften
5. Next add parsley, basil, wine and capers
6. Cook fish on top of mixture
7. Squeeze lemon over fish and add salt and pepper
8. Cook until done with a cover (about 10 minutes)
9. Simmer for 5 more minutes and serve over rice if desired

Spicy Garlic Fish

6 crushed cloves of garlic

2 T ground cumin

2 T cayenne pepper

lemon juice

1 ½ lbs cod

1 can of tomato paste (6oz)

olive oil

½ cup water

optional- 2 long hot peppers

1. Using a small bowl, make a paste with the garlic, cumin, pepper and a splash of lemon juice to blend
2. Heat oil in a medium frying pan (use enough oil to cover bottom of pan)
3. Add ½ the paste and ½ the can of tomato paste (save the other half of each for next time)
4. Cover and cook on low until cooked well (1/2 hour)
5. Stir occasionally with a spatula and add 2 long hot peppers if desired (cook until soft)
6. Add water and simmer-mix frequently until smooth (about ½ hour)
7. Cut up fish into serving pieces and put in spooning mixture over fish
8. Cook on low/medium for 10 minutes or until fish flakes apart
9. Keep covered until ready to serve (great with bread or bagels)

Sweet and Spicy Fish

1 ½ lbs cod

1 T sesame oil

½ cup honey

¼ cup soy sauce

juice of 1 lemon or lemon juice equivalent

crushed red pepper flakes

black pepper

2 crushed garlic cloves

sesame seeds

1. Blend marinade ingredients
2. Pour over fish-use large glass pan
3. Sprinkle sesame seeds over top of fish
4. Cover with plastic wrap and marinate in refrigerator for several hours or overnight
5. Bake at 375 degrees for 30 minutes or until done (fish flakes easily with a fork)
6. Extra spicy-if desired add additional black and red pepper over fish before baking